To my family; you're what's important —L.S.N.

For firefighters everywhere —E.R.

Owlkids Books acknowledges the financial support of the Canada Council for the Arts, the Ontario Arts Council, the Government of Canada through the Canada Book Fund (CBF), and the Government of Ontario through the Ontario Creates Book Initiative for our publishing activities.

Owlkids Books gratefully acknowledges that our office in Toronto is located on the traditional territory of many nations, including the Mississaugas of the Credit, the Chippewa, the Wendat, the Anishinaabeg, and the Haudenosaunee Peoples.

Published in Canada by Owlkids Books Inc.
1 Eglinton Avenue East, Toronto, ON, M4P 3A1

Published in the US by Owlkids Books Inc.
1700 Fourth Street, Berkeley, CA, 94710

Library of Congress Control Number: 2022937967

Library and Archives Canada Cataloguing in Publication

Title: What to bring / written by Lorna Schultz Nicholson ; illustrated by Ellen Rooney.
Names: Schultz Nicholson, Lorna, author. | Rooney, Ellen, illustrator.
Identifiers: Canadiana 20220224307 | ISBN 9781771474900 (hardcover)
Classification: LCC PS8637.C58 W53 2023 | DDC jC813/.6—dc23

Edited by Jennifer Stokes
Designed by Alisa Baldwin

Manufactured in Shenzhen, Guangdong, China, in September 2022, by WKT Co. Ltd.
Job # 22CB0152

MIX
Paper from responsible sources
FSC® C104723

A   B   C   D   E   F

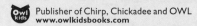

Publisher of Chirp, Chickadee and OWL
www.owlkidsbooks.com

Owlkids Books is a division of bayard canada

ONTARIO ARTS COUNCIL
CONSEIL DES ARTS DE L'ONTARIO
an Ontario government agency
un organisme du gouvernement de l'Ontario

Canada Council for the Arts   Conseil des Arts du Canada

Canada

What to Bring

Written by
Lorna Schultz Nicholson

Illustrated by
Ellen Rooney

OWLKIDS BOOKS

MALIA LOOKS AT THE SKY. She sees a huge white-and-gray cloud.

Something smells.

"That's smoke!" says Mama.

Malia watches loud planes fly into the cloud of smoke.

Mama talks to the neighbors.

The cloud of smoke grows.

"We should go inside," says Mama.

Soon after they get into the house, someone bangs on the front door.

Mama speaks to a woman in a brightly colored vest.

Malia hides behind Mama's legs.

Then Daddy comes home—
and it isn't even dinnertime.

"What's happening?" Malia asks.

"We have to leave the house, just to be safe," says Mama.
"The fire is getting close."

Mama throws Jackson's blankie in a suitcase.

Daddy folds up Jackson's stroller.

Malia hides behind the sofa.

"Malia, come out from there," says Daddy softly.

"I want to take my things too," says Malia.

"What would you like to bring?" Daddy asks.

"I want to bring my tree fort."

Daddy shakes his head. "It's too big."

"My sandbox?"

"Still too big," says Daddy. "Pick small toys. Things important to you."

Malia goes to her room. What should she bring?

Everything!

She starts a pile.

Rabbit and Turtle.

Blankets and pillows and books.

LOTS of books.

Her family of teddy bears.

Then Mama is at her door.
"Malia, we can't take all that."

"But it's *all* important!"

"Three things," says Mama.
"And put the rest in your heart."

Malia doesn't want to choose.

She sits on her bed, trying to decide. If she brings only Turtle, Rabbit will be sad.

Daddy hurries by her door, and Chester runs behind him.

Malia hears Jackson asking for his bottle and Snowball meowing.

"Are you ready, Malia?" Mama asks in her hurry-up voice.

Malia nods.

"Put your three things in your backpack."

But Malia shakes her head. "My backpack is too small for what I want to bring," she says.

Then she whispers in Mama's ear.

Daddy carries Jackson.

Malia walks Chester.

Mama wrestles Snowball into her carrier
and turns off the lights.

As they drive away from the house, Malia presses her
face to the window. Outside, she sees orange flames in the
distance and a sky that is no longer blue.

Inside the car, Mama drives while
Daddy calls Grandpa.

Jackson drinks his bottle.

Chester pants.

Snowball meows.

Malia knows she brought what is important.